the SMURFS™

Why Do You Cry, Baby Smurf?

by Peyo

Ready-to-Read

Simon Spotlight

New York   London   Toronto   Sydney   New Delhi

SIMON SPOTLIGHT
An imprint of Simon & Schuster Children's Publishing Division
1230 Avenue of the Americas, New York, New York 10020
© Peyo - 2013 - Licensed through Lafig Belgium - www.smurf.com. All Rights Reserved.
Originally published in French in 2003 as *Bébé pleure* written by Peyo.
English language translation copyright © 2013 by Peyo. All rights reserved.
Translated by Elizabeth Dennis Barton
All rights reserved, including the right of reproduction in whole or in part in any form.
SIMON SPOTLIGHT, READY-TO-READ, and colophon are registered
trademarks of Simon & Schuster, Inc.
For information about special discounts for bulk purchases,
please contact Simon & Schuster Special Sales at
1-866-506-1949 or business@simonandschuster.com.
The Simon & Schuster Speakers Bureau can bring authors to your live event.
For more information or to book an event contact the Simon & Schuster Speakers Bureau
at 1-866-248-3049 or visit our website at www.simonspeakers.com
Manufactured in the United States of America 1112 LAK
First Edition
1 2 3 4 5 6 7 8 9 10
ISBN 978-1-4424-6191-8 (pbk)
ISBN 978-1-4424-6193-2 (hc)

"Rise and shine," Smurfette said, one bright and sunny morning. Baby Smurf giggled and reached his arms out to her.

Smurfette gave Baby Smurf a bath. He played with his rubber ducky and splashed water everywhere. "I really should have smurfed my swim trunks," whined Vanity Smurf.

After his bath, Smurfette carried
Baby Smurf over to his toys so
he could play. He stopped smiling.
"What's the matter?"
asked Smurfette.

And that's when Baby Smurf started to cry. He cried so loudly that everyone in Smurf Village heard him. All the Smurfs came running over.

"Maybe he can't find one of his toys," said Brainy Smurf.
Brainy picked up a teddy bear and showed it to him.
"Is this the toy you want?"
But Baby Smurf only cried louder.

The Smurfs searched and searched
for a toy that would make
Baby Smurf stop crying, but
nothing worked.

Then Brainy had another idea.
"Maybe we can calm him down
if we give him some sweets!"
Brainy told Smurfette.
But today, Baby Smurf didn't
even want sweets!

Poor Cook Smurf! He tried to help
by bringing over an ice-cream cone
with Baby Smurf's favorite flavors:
vanilla, raspberry, and smurfberry.
But Baby Smurf pushed it back
into Cook Smurf's face!

"He must be sick," said Smurfette.
"Let's bring him to Papa Smurf.
He'll be able to figure out what
is wrong."

Papa Smurf examined Baby Smurf. "He doesn't have a fever," said Papa. "Or any spots or rashes. And it doesn't seem like he has a stomachache." Papa thought for a moment. "I bet he has a new baby tooth smurfing in! Take him for a walk. That will calm him down."

So Smurfette, Vanity, and Brainy
went for a walk with Baby Smurf.
At first, Baby Smurf was quiet.

But when they came to the pond,
they saw some ducks swimming by,
and Baby Smurf started to cry again.
"I don't understand," said Smurfette.
"He usually adores ducks!"

The group returned to Smurf
Village and put Baby Smurf in his
sandbox. But he kept crying.
"I don't know what he wants,"
Smurfette said with a sigh.
"I give up."

The Smurfs couldn't take
Baby Smurf's crying anymore.
One Smurf got a headache,
and another put earplugs in his ears.
Finally, a Smurf said,
"We have to do something!"

So Harmony Smurf took out his trumpet.

"No!" yelled a Smurf.

Whenever Harmony played the trumpet, his music made everyone want to cry.

Jokey Smurf put on his clown suit.
He hoped his clown jokes would
make Baby Smurf laugh,
but the baby didn't stop crying.
That made Jokey start to cry.

"I'll make Baby Smurf happy again," said Clumsy Smurf. "Ready for some juggling?" But Baby Smurf never even cracked a smile. . . .

Not even when all the balls
landed on Clumsy's head.
Thunk! Thunk! Thunk! Thunk!

Next the Smurfs put on a puppet show for Baby Smurf. Usually he loved the story of Little Red Riding Smurf, but not today.
He kept crying!

The Smurfs kept on trying to make
Baby Smurf happy. They then
opened up the doors of the shed.
"Come on, everyone, smurf
together!" cried Handy Smurf.

With a little effort, the Smurfs pulled the merry-go-round out of the shed. Handy was happy to turn it on. Maybe this would be the thing to make Baby Smurf stop crying!

But it was no use! As he sat on the ducky seat on the merry-go-round, Baby Smurf began to cry again. The Smurfs shook their heads sadly. "We have smurfed all we can," said one of the Smurfs. "Nothing will make Baby Smurf happy today."

Smurfette scooped Baby Smurf
up in her arms. "I'll just bring him
back to the house and smurf him
to bed. Maybe he'll tire himself
out from all the crying and just fall
asleep," she said hopefully.

As Smurfette pushed the baby
carriage up to her house,
an amazing thing happened.
Baby Smurf began to laugh!

Baby Smurf laughed some more as
Smurfette walked toward the yard.
"What could be making him laugh?"
Smurfette asked herself.
Then she saw his ducky inner tube.
Baby Smurf had used it the day
before when they went swimming
in the lake!

When Smurfette gave Baby Smurf his ducky, he hugged it and wouldn't let it go. "All day you wanted your ducky so you could go swimming like you did yesterday," said Smurfette.

So Smurfette took Baby Smurf
back to the lake. He laughed and
laughed and laughed as he paddled
in the water in his ducky. And as
Hefty watched over Baby Smurf,
Smurfette finally got a
chance to rest!

But not for long! "There's a hole
in the inner tube!" yelled Hefty.
"Quick! Call Handy Smurf so he can
smurf a patch to fix it. Otherwise
Baby Smurf will start to cry again!"